POWER CODERS

THE BEST-SELLING APP

ADAM FURGANG

ILLUSTRATED BY JOEL GENNARI

PowerKiDS press

New York

Published in 2021 by The Rosen Publishing Group, Inc.
29 East 21st Street, New York, NY 10010

First Edition

Illustrator: Joel Gennari
Interior Layout: Tanya Dellaccio
Editorial Director: Greg Roza
Colorist: SirGryphon
Coding Consultant: Caleb Stone

Library of Congress Cataloging-in-Publication Data
Names: Furgang, Adam, author. | Gennari, Joel, illustrator.
Title: The best-selling app / Adam Furgang ; illustrated by Joel Gennari.
Description: New York : PowerKids Press, [2021] | Series: Power coders |
Includes index. | Summary: After his Young Entrepreneur's Club meeting,
Peter excitedly tells Naya, Grace, and Tommy several ideas he has and
presses the Power Coders to help him invent a killer app.
Identifiers: LCCN 2019038964 | ISBN 9781725307681 (paperback) | ISBN
9781725307704 (library binding) | ISBN 9781725307711 (ebook) | ISBN
9781725307698 Subjects: LCSH: Graphic novels. | CYAC: Graphic novels. |
Application software–Fiction. | Computer programming–Fiction.
Classification: LCC PZ7.7.F86 Be 2020 | DDC 741.5/973–dc23
LC record available at https://lccn.loc.gov/2019038964

Manufactured in the United States of America

CPSIA Compliance Information: Batch CSPK20. For Further Information contact Rosen Publishing, New York, New York at 1-800-237-9932.

CONTENTS

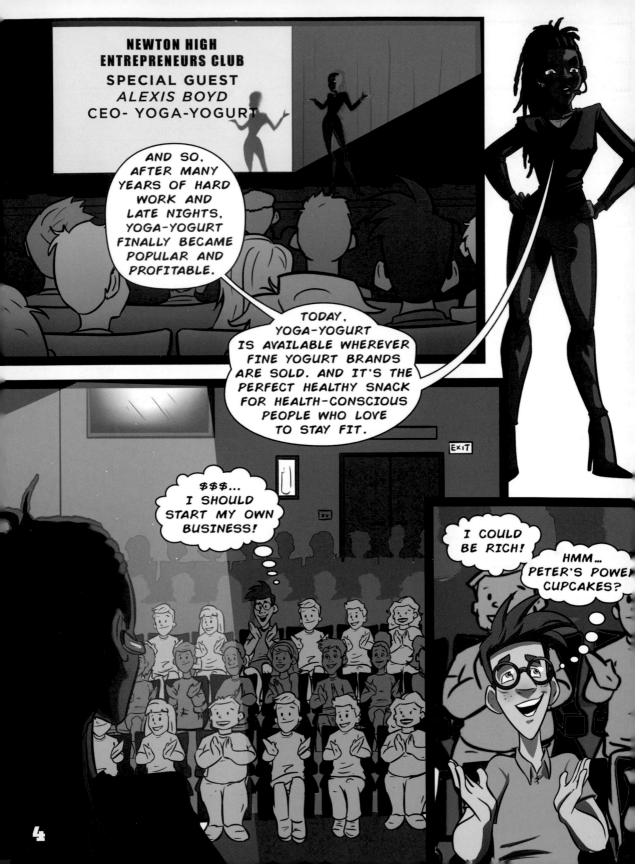

MS. BOYD. HI!

I'M PETER.

I WAS AT THE ENTREPRENEURS CLUB MEETING THE OTHER DAY, AND I WAS VERY INSPIRED BY YOUR STORY AND YOGA-YOGURT.

THANK YOU.

IT'S NICE TO MEET YOU, PETER.

MY FRIENDS AND I HAVE THIS CLUB, THE POWER CODERS.

AND WE'RE TRYING TO THINK OF A GREAT IDEA FOR A BUSINESS OF OUR OWN.

BUT WE'RE ALL BUSY WORKING THIS SUMMER AND IT'S GOING TO BE TOUGH TO FIND TIME TO HANG OUT.

AND WITH NO FREE TIME, WE WON'T BE ABLE TO COME UP WITH A GREAT IDEA FOR A BUSINESS OR A GREAT APP, LET ALONE START ONE.

8

THEN, WHEN I'M NOT CLEANING POOLS, I CAN FIND SOME TIME TO HANG WITH ALL OF YOU.

I HOPE!

YOU MIGHT NOT ALWAYS FIND TIME TO GET TOGETHER, BUT IT SHOULD MAKE MEETING SIMPLER.

THE PROGRAM DOESN'T NEED TO BE FANCY. OR PRETTY.

IT DOESN'T NEED TO BE PRETTY TO START ...

BUT I CAN BEGIN WORKING ON SOME DESIGNS AND LOGOS ANYWAY.

WE CAN ALL SPLIT THE WORK AND HAVE A SIMPLE WEB VERSION OF SCHEDULE-SYNC READY BEFORE SCHOOL ENDS.

LET'S MEET AGAIN AT LUNCH.

THE NEXT DAY

THE PORTABLE HARD DRIVE WITH THE SCHEDULE-SYNC CODE STOPPED WORKING AND MY COMPUTER WON'T READ IT.

I TESTED IT ON THREE OTHER COMPUTERS THIS MORNING.

IT DIDN'T WORK ON ANY OF THEM.

PLEASE TELL ME YOU HAVE A BACKUP.

UH... NOPE.

I DIDN'T THINK OF IT.

SINCE WE'VE BEEN WORKING TOGETHER, I JUST WORKED OFF THE HARD DRIVE, TOO.

MAYBE THE USB CABLE IS BAD?

I THOUGHT OF THAT.

I TESTED IT WITH CABLES THAT WORKED ON OTHER COMPUTERS. NO LUCK.

WHAT'S UP?

WE LOST OUR CODE FOR THE SCHEDULE-SYNC APP.

I CAN'T BELIEVE WE FORGOT TO BACK UP OUR FILES.

AND NOW THE PORTABLE HARD DRIVE ISN'T WORKING. EVEN AFTER I TESTED IT ON THREE DIFFERENT COMPUTERS WITH DIFFERENT CABLES.

THERE MUST BE SOMETHING WE CAN DO.

WE ONLY HAVE A WEEK BEFORE SCHOOL ENDS.

AND TOMMY AND I WON'T HAVE ENOUGH TIME TO WRITE NEW CODE TO HAVE SCHEDULE-SYNC READY BEFORE WE ALL START WORKING NEXT WEEK.

23

27

28

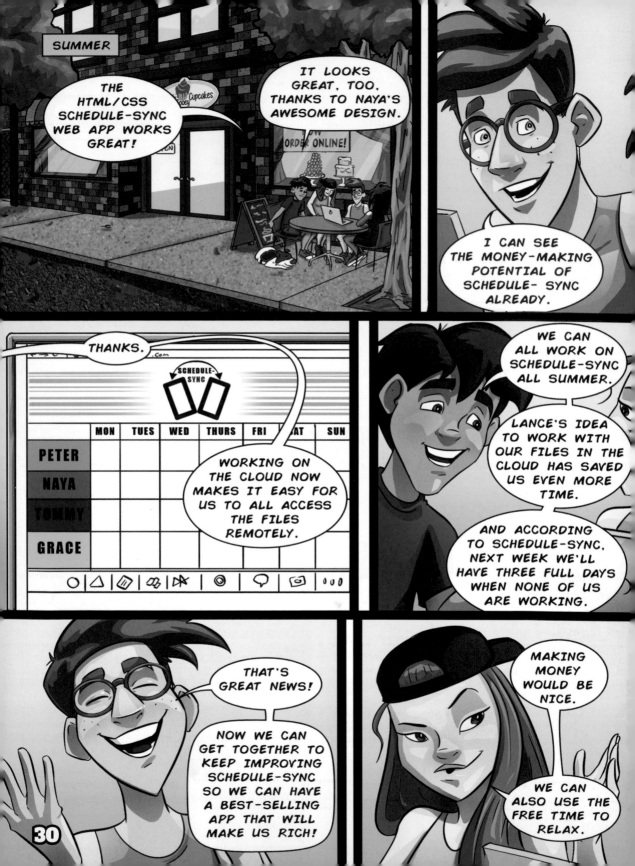

SUMMER

THE HTML/CSS SCHEDULE-SYNC WEB APP WORKS GREAT!

IT LOOKS GREAT, TOO, THANKS TO NAYA'S AWESOME DESIGN.

I CAN SEE THE MONEY-MAKING POTENTIAL OF SCHEDULE-SYNC ALREADY.

THANKS.

SCHEDULE-SYNC

	MON	TUES	WED	THURS	FRI	SAT	SUN
PETER							
NAYA							
TOMMY							
GRACE							

WORKING ON THE CLOUD NOW MAKES IT EASY FOR US TO ALL ACCESS THE FILES REMOTELY.

WE CAN ALL WORK ON SCHEDULE-SYNC ALL SUMMER.

LANCE'S IDEA TO WORK WITH OUR FILES IN THE CLOUD HAS SAVED US EVEN MORE TIME.

AND ACCORDING TO SCHEDULE-SYNC, NEXT WEEK WE'LL HAVE THREE FULL DAYS WHEN NONE OF US ARE WORKING.

THAT'S GREAT NEWS!

NOW WE CAN GET TOGETHER TO KEEP IMPROVING SCHEDULE-SYNC SO WE CAN HAVE A BEST-SELLING APP THAT WILL MAKE US RICH!

MAKING MONEY WOULD BE NICE.

WE CAN ALSO USE THE FREE TIME TO RELAX.

30